CALLING ALL
MASTER BUILDERS!

LONDON, NEW YORK, MUNICH,
MELBOURNE AND DELHI

Editor David Fentiman
Senior Editor Helen Murray
Project Art Editor Lauren Rosier
Pre-Production Producer
Mark Staples
Producer Louise Minihane
Managing Editor Elizabeth Dowsett
Design Manager Ron Stobbart
Publishing Manager Julie Ferris
Art Director Lisa Lanzarini
Publishing Director Simon Beecroft

Reading Consultant Maureen Fernandes

The LEGO® Movie screenplay by
Phil Lord and Christopher Miller

The LEGO® Movie story by
Dan Hageman & Kevin Hageman
and Phil Lord & Christopher Miller

Dorling Kindersley would like to thank Randi Sørensen
and Matthew James Ashton at the LEGO Group.

First published in Great Britain in 2014 by
Dorling Kindersley Limited
80 Strand, London WC2R 0RL

10 9 8 7 6 5 4 3 2 1
001–193756–Jan/14

Page design copyright © 2014 Dorling Kindersley Limited,
A Penguin Random House Company

A CIP catalogue record for this book
is available from the British Library.

ISBN: 978-1-40934-169-7

Colour reproduction by Altaimage, UK
Printed and bound in the Slovak Republic by TBB, a. s.

Discover more at
www.dk.com
www.LEGO.com

Contents

CALLING ALL
MASTER BUILDERS!

DAVID FENTIMAN

Vitruvius

This blind wizard is Vitruvius.
He is ancient and very wise.

Sparkling
cape

4

Vitruvius used to look after a mysterious object called the Kragle.

A powerful man called Lord Business has stolen the Kragle. He is using it in his evil plans.

Staff

Kragle

The Master Builders

Vitruvius is a Master Builder.

Master Builders have the power to build anything they can imagine.

The Master Builders must hide from Lord Business and his army of police robots.

Lord Business

Lord Business is very mean!
He plans to use the Kragle
to glue the whole
world together!

He is hunting the Master
Builders because they want
to stop his plans.

Giant ——————————
legs

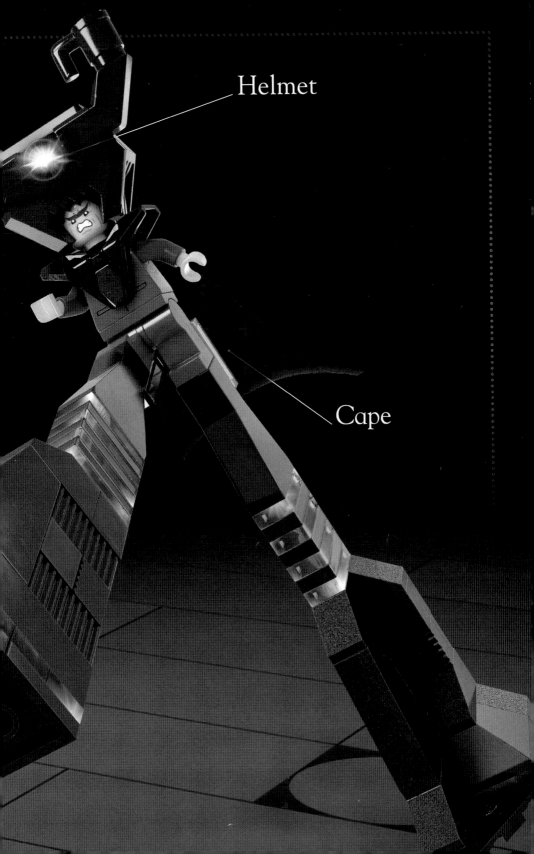

Helmet

Cape

The Special

Vitruvius said that the greatest Master Builder would rise up and defeat Lord Business.

This Master Builder would be called the Special.

Who do you think it will be?
Could it be one
of these people
from the city
of Bricksburg?

The Special

?

Amazing Builders

The Master Builders
all look different.
They can build all kinds
of incredible things.

Punk Rocker

Let's meet
some of them!

Yeti

Could one of these
be the Special?

Can they help to
stop Lord Business?

Artist

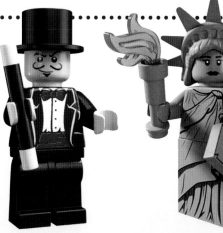
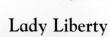

Hazmat Guy   Magician   Lady Liberty

Marsha   Shakespeare

Abraham   Circus
Lincoln   Clown

Meet Emmet

This happy man is Emmet.
He is a builder who
lives in Bricksburg.
Emmet always tries to
follow instructions.

He doesn't know about
Lord Business, the Master
Builders, or the
Special – yet.

Instructions

Badge

The Piece of Resistance

A mysterious object has become stuck to Emmet's back.

Piece of
Resistance

It is the Piece of Resistance!
The Piece is the only thing
that can stop the Kragle.

This means that Emmet is
the Special!

Can Emmet really defeat
Lord Business?

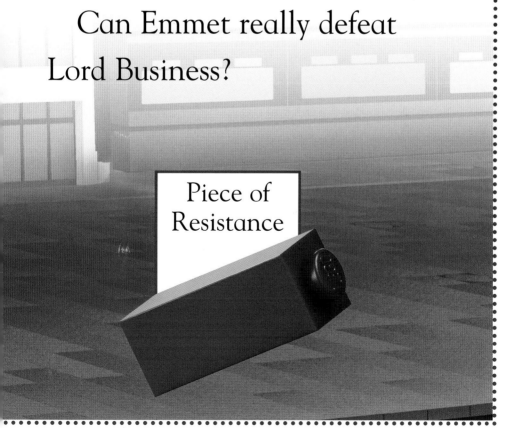

Piece of
Resistance

Wyldstyle

Wyldstyle is one of the bravest Master Builders. She will help Emmet on his quest.

Wyldstyle is amazing at building things. She is also very good at rescuing Emmet.

Emmet thinks she is very pretty.

Sword

Batman

This is Batman.

He is Wyldstyle's boyfriend.

Batman is a super hero
and a Master Builder.

He flies a plane
called the Batwing.

He saves Wyldstyle
and Emmet when they
are in trouble.

Bat
symbol

Unikitty

Unikitty is a Master Builder.
She is also princess of a magical
place called Cloud Cuckoo Land.

Unikitty is half unicorn
and half kitty.

She turns into Angry Kitty
when she is very angry!

Angry Kitty

MetalBeard

MetalBeard is
a pirate and a
Master Builder.

He isn't an
ordinary pirate.
His body is made of bits of ships!

MetalBeard lost his body in
a battle against Lord Business.

Benny

Benny is a spaceman.
He likes building spaceships
more than anything else.

He is a Master Builder
so he is really good at
making spaceships.

Benny is from the 1980s.
He sometimes struggles
with new technology.

Cracked
helmet

Bad Cop

Bad Cop has been sent by
Lord Business to hunt down
the Master Builders.

Megaphone

He flies a Jet-Car to
look for Emmet and
the Piece of Resistance.

He wants to stop
Emmet from ruining
Lord Business's plan.

Jet-Car

Working together

Now that they know Emmet is the Special, all of the Master Builders must work together.

They must help Emmet put the Piece of Resistance on the Kragle to disarm it. Only this will defeat Lord Business – and save the world!

Glossary

Kragle
A mysterious object that can glue things.

The Special
The greatest of the Master Builders.

Piece of Resistance
The Piece fits on to the Kragle and stops it.

Angry Kitty
What Unikitty looks like when she is angry.

Jet-Car
Bad Cop's vehicle.

Index